Crash at Sea

Margaret Scariano

A **HIGH ADVENTURE** BOOK
High Noon Books
Novato, California

Cover Design: Jim McConnell
Interior Illustrations: Herb Heidinger

International Standard Book Number: 0-87879-408-5

10 09 08 07 06 05 04 03 02
15 14 13 12 11 10

High Noon Books

a division of ATP
20 Commercial Blvd.
Novato, California 94949

Contents

Chapter 1

Wanted: A Shipmate

Brett Hampton stood on the dock. Again he looked at his watch. Late! One thing he knew. If Peggy was going to be his sailing partner, she'd have to be on time. Eight bells meant eight bells!

With his finger he shoved his glasses up on the bridge of his nose. Most of the time he didn't mind wearing glasses. After all, he was a reader — and a pretty fair student. Not some big football hero. But contact lens would sure be great for sailing.

Brett looked out across the bay. The sky was blue. The breezes were soft. And the waves rolled gently to shore. Then his eyes searched the dock. Still no Peggy. He was sure he'd told her eight o'clock. He could even remember the sound of her voice. "Eight o'clock," she'd repeated in her soft voice. Her voice was what made him notice her in the first place. He'd been having lunch in

1

the cafeteria. The place was crowded. The table behind him was noisy. Suddenly, through all the racket he heard a voice—soft but clear. He'd turned around on the bench and looked.

Her small figure was the second thing he noticed. She was the right size—not too heavy. But not too light. Just right!

Ever since his friend Ernie had moved away, Brett had been looking for just the right shipmate. He needed one for the Summer Bay Sailboat Race. He'd never thought about having a girl as shipmate. But why not? Peggy was on the soft ball team. He'd seen her play tennis. Then just last Wednesday, he'd watched her in her gymnastics class. She did somersaults and hand springs, and stood on her head on the high bar. She had looked strong and sure of herself.

So he had asked her to go sailing with him this Saturday. Peggy had seemed surprised. He remembered how she held her breath and then said, "Sailing? With you?" Then she swallowed and said, "Yes."

Brett walked toward the street. Maybe she was waiting on the boardwalk. She *was* kind of "spacey." She talked and laughed all the time. But maybe she didn't listen carefully. That was the trouble about needing a partner. It was hard to depend on someone else.

With Ernie it had been different. They each did a job and worked together. What a team! Brett was sure they would have won the race this year. Together their weight was right. The sailboat was in perfect shape. They had sailed together so much, they did what needed to be done without talking about it.

Then he saw her. She was running toward the dock. But what a sight! Brett didn't know whether to laugh or pretend he didn't know her.

"Hi! Brett!" She raised her hand to wave. The life preserver around her middle started to slide. She let go of her sailor hat and grabbed at the life preserver. Too late. The hat bounced off and rolled down the boardwalk. The life preserver fell around her ankles. She grabbed a pole to keep from falling.

Good grief! This couldn't be the Peggy Drake who did so well in sports. This gal looked like an accident waiting to happen.

He hoped no one who knew him was around. He'd be laughed right off the dock. He looked again and closed his eyes. He must be dreaming. No one would wear both a Mae West life vest *and* a donut-shaped life preserver *AND* on dry land! And she also had on underwater goggles!

He opened his eyes again. It was no dream. Peggy looked like somebody from outer space.

"Sorry I'm late, Brett." She sounded out of breath. I couldn't reach my Mae West life vest. Then I climbed on my dresser to get the vest off the top shelf and stepped on my sun glasses. Yep, smashed them to bits." She lifted her small

The life preserver fell around her ankles.

4

shoulders in a tiny shrug. "So here I am at last. I borrowed my brother's underwater goggles. Wind makes my eyes water." She looked around. "Where's the ship?"

"Ship? Oh, you mean my sailboat. At the end of the dock." Brett stepped in front of Peggy. "I'll lead the way." Maybe no one will think she's with me, he thought.

"Aye, aye, my captain." Peggy followed right behind him. She was so close that the donut-shaped life preserver poked him in the back.

Brett walked faster. At the end of the dock he stopped. "Here we are. Give me your hand. I'll help you."

Peggy stood there. "This is the ship we're going in? I mean, it looks so small. Small for a big ocean and everything."

"It's safe. I've sailed in it for years. Maybe you'd be more comfortable if you took off the vest or the life preserver. One kind of life preserver should be enough."

"I need all the help I can get. If that boat turns over, I'll faint. Just thinking about whales and sharks and eels gives me the creeps."

"Hey, Peggy, you're not really scared, are you? You're just putting me on. Right?"

"Wrong. I'm terrified."

Chapter 2

Stuck with a "Landlubber"

Brett's mouth dropped open. His insides felt as heavy as an anchor. "You mean—you mean you're afraid of water?"

"Terrified is the word. I don't even dip my big toe into a wading pool without a life preserver."

"But you're tops in sports at school."

Peggy smiled. "Yes, that's true. But that doesn't mean I'm tops in *every* sport. I mean I can swim. I can dog paddle—if you call that swimming. But I've never, never been boating before." She looked at him. "Or do I mean never been shipping before?"

Oh no! A real zero! Brett's hopes for a sailing partner in Peggy died.

"And the ocean—I guess I didn't think it was so big," Peggy said.

"But why did you agree to come sailing today? I just don't get it." Brett didn't want to be mean.

But darn! He'd wasted a perfectly good Saturday. Wasted it on a girl who didn't even like the water.

Peggy reached out and touched his arm. "Because I thought it would be fun to be with you."

That was the last thing Brett had expected to hear. He frowned at Peggy. Then he started to laugh.

"What's so funny?" Peggy asked. Her green-blue eyes were the color of the sea.

"Us. We're some pair. We've been playing games with each other."

"What do you mean—playing games? I'm not sure I like that." Peggy sounded hurt. She looked down at the ground. Then she looked up at him again. "I just thought it would be nice to get to know you. I guess I was wrong." She turned and started toward the boardwalk.

"Hey, wait. I didn't mean to make you mad. I guess I was playing a game, too."

Peggy stopped and turned around. "Honest? You really were, Brett?"

"Sure. I asked you because I needed a partner for the sailboat race. You're good in sports. And the right size."

Peggy laughed. "Now I understand. You asked

me out because you thought I could help in the race. And I said yes because I thought we would go to a movie or a football game or something. You're right, Brett, we *were* playing games with one another."

"So what are we going to do?" Brett asked. He sure didn't want to waste a whole day.

Peggy grinned. "Do? We're going sailing. Give me a hand." She took a step toward the sailboat. It rocked gently from side to side.

"Give me the life preserver. I'll hand it to you when you're seated. Don't worry. The life vest will keep you afloat." Brett laid the preserver on the deck. He grabbed Peggy's arm and helped her into the sailboat. She looked tense. But she was in the boat.

"OK?" Brett asked. Peggy nodded. He handed her the life preserver. She put it on the seat next to her. Then he untied the rope from the dock and hopped in the boat. The boat slowly drifted away from the dock.

Brett took her hand. "Come on. I'll show you around." They went down a few steps to the tiny galley where meals were fixed.

There were two bunks for sleeping. A closet held life preservers, flares, first-aid equipment, and a two-way radio. Top-side there were deck chairs and a small table with a folded umbrella.

"Just like home," Brett said. "Why don't you sit here while I set us on our course?"

Peggy sat in the deck chair. The underwater goggles hung around her neck. Her hands gripped the arm rests. Her knuckles were white.

Brett patted her shoulder. "Take it easy, sport. I'm going to set the sails. We'll head for Shepherd Island. That's not too far."

Peggy's laugh was shaky. "Not too far? I guess not. But to me Shepherd Island looks like it's on the edge of the world."

When Brett returned, Peggy seemed more relaxed. Her fingers no longer gripped the arm rests. The life preserver was against the side of the boat. Brett said, "Come back here. I'll show you how we steer the sailboat."

Peggy sat next to Brett on the seat. He showed her how moving the tiller changed the course of the sailboat.

"Here, you try it." He put her hand on the tiller.

The sails billowed in the sea breeze. "How beautiful the sails are." Peggy turned and smiled at him. "It's like being pulled by white, fluffy clouds."

The boat held its course for the far side of

Shepherd Island.

"I can't believe I'm doing this," Peggy said. The breeze swept her hair back from her face. "I'm having fun."

Brett took the tiller and headed for the far side of the island. He ran the boat up on the sandy beach. Then he helped Peggy get out.

"I feel like I'm still on the water. My legs feel funny," Peggy said.

Brett laughed. "You'll get your land legs back pretty quick. How about over by that large rock? Think that'd be a good place for lunch?"

Brett carried the picnic basket. Peggy took off her Mae West life vest and laid it on the sandy beach. "Guess I won't need these either." She laid the goggles on top of the vest.

"Come on. We'll build a fire over there in those rocks." Brett took Peggy's hand.

It was hard walking on the beach. Just a few steps on the beach filled their shoes with sand.

"Hey, hold it, sailor." Peggy stopped. Hanging on to Brett's arm, she took off her shoes. She wiggled her toes in the warm sand. "There. That's better."

"Good idea." Brett set the picnic basket down and took off his shoes. He tied the laces together and hung the shoes around his neck. Then they ran toward the ring of rocks.

"You spread out the picnic gear. I'll gather some driftwood for a fire." Brett headed down the beach.

Peggy spread out a red-checked cloth on the sand. She took out the hot dogs and the buns. They'd need a couple of long sticks to roast weenies. She looked around and spotted some slender branches. Someone else had enjoyed a weenie roast, she thought. The sticks were charred on the end.

By the time Brett returned with the driftwood Peggy had the potato salad, celery and carrots, and a bag of marshmallows set out.

Quickly Brett started the fire and soon they were roasting the hot dogs. "One more, Peggy, or are you ready for dessert? The fire looks just right for toasting marshmallows."

"Just one marshmallow, Brett. I'm stuffed."

"Want another soda?" Brett asked.

"No thanks. I'll pop if I eat one more thing." Peggy leaned against the huge rock. Then she said, "I'm glad I didn't back out, Brett. This has really been fun. I didn't know what I was missing."

Brett said, "Good for you, Peggy. You don't give up. I watched you play baseball last week.

You hung in there until the bottom of the ninth and the third strike-out. I like that."

Peggy stood up and brushed the sand from her clothes. "After today I might go in for sailing. It's a lot of fun."

"Speaking of sailing." Brett looked at his watch. "We'd better be heading back to shore."

They packed the leftover food in the picnic basket and carried it back to the boat. Peggy put on her Mae West life vest again. She sat down in a deck chair. Brett rolled up his pants legs. He waded into the water and shoved the boat from the sandy beach. Then he jumped aboard.

They sailed around the island to head for shore. But there was no shore in sight. Suddenly there was nothing but thick fog all around them.

Chapter 3

Lost in the Fog

Brett heard Peggy cry out. But from the moment they had left the island, fog blocked out everything. Now he couldn't even see her. "Take it easy, Peggy. Just a little patch of fog. We'll sail right out of it. You'll see."

"How could it be? Just a moment ago it was sunny skies and now — now we're wrapped in this gray blanket." Peggy's voice sounded high and funny. Like she was really scared and trying to bluff it out. Brett tried to see through the fog. Nothing!

"The air has turned cool. Guess I'll put my sweater on. If I can find it," Peggy said.

"Don't stand up, Peggy. If you fell overboard, I'd never find you in this fog."

"Don't even think such a thing, Brett Hampton. What's that sound?"

"Just the waves lapping against the sides of the

boat. I haven't started the motor yet. Thought I'd better wait until I could see a little better." Brett tried to make his voice sound cheerful. But he didn't like being out in the fog either. It was like being blindfolded. All sense of direction got turned around.

"We're lost. Right?" Peggy whispered. "It's all right. You can tell me. I won't lose control." She tried to laugh as she added, "And I certainly won't jump overboard. All the sharks and whales and eels just waiting to touch me. Yuk!"

Their shoulders were touching, and Brett could feel her shudder. "Hey, lighten up. I know you were great in sports events. But I didn't know you were into drama, too. On the bay, fog is not unusual."

"I'm sorry, Brett. But I'm used to being in control of my life. And—and out here I'm not." Her voice shook. "Are we lost? Don't kid me. I can take it."

Brett was quiet a moment. He knew Peggy was scared. He heard it in her voice. In the way she talked so fast. He needed to give her something to do. Something that would take her mind off the fog. But what?

"Peggy, calm down. We might be delayed a little bit by the fog. But just think of the great story you can tell. Instead of the 'we ran out of gas' oldie, you'll have a new excuse for being late. 'We ran into fog.' " Brett laughed but Peggy's laugh sounded more like a whimper.

"I wish I were on dry land right now. I feel like I'm wrapped in a damp sheet." Peggy's voice sounded like a little girl's.

"One time Ernie and I got caught in the fog off Point Lucky," Brett said.

"How long were you lost?" Peggy asked.

"Not too long. Fog's funny. It can drift in fast and disappear just as quickly. The day Ernie and I got caught off Point Lucky, I was sleeping. Ernie was at the tiller. Suddenly I heard Ernie calling me. I ran top-side. The fog was so thick, I couldn't even see Ernie."

"What did you do?" Peggy asked.

"What any red-blooded sailor would do. I yelled. Which scared Ernie." Brett laughed as he remembered. "He jumped up and grabbed me. I thought he was going to throw me overboard."

"Why?" Peggy asked.

"Well, Ernie was big on monsters. He believed in the Loch Ness monster and other sea serpents. He said he looked up and saw a shadowy figure. Then he heard me yell. He was sure I was an underwater sea monster."

"What about the fog?"

"Nothing to it," Brett said. "We'd sailed into the fog. So all we did was turn around and sail out of it."

"It might have worked then. But now it's different. We're surrounded by fog. Are we going around in circles? I mean, that's what people do when they're lost on land," Peggy said.

"No. I have a compass and map. Getting lost is not the problem," Brett said. Then he knew what Peggy could do. It would help him. But it would also make her feel as if she were doing something to help, too.

"Want me to steer while you look at the maps?" Peggy asked.

"No, but I'll tell you what you can do. And it would help a lot. Keep a watch at the bow of the boat for any other boats."

"OK. Do I just yell out if I see something?"

"Right." Brett watched her shadowy figure stand. In seconds he could no longer see her form. Then she called out.

"All set, Brett. Don't worry. I'll keep a sharp eye out."

Brett smiled to himself. Already her voice sounded better.

"I'm going to blow the fog horn, Peggy. So

don't be scared." Brett squeezed the bulb of the horn several times. Its lonely sound filled the foggy air.

"You seem so far away, Brett. Are you sure your boat isn't growing longer?" Peggy asked.

Brett laughed. "Nope. It's just the fog. It makes everything seem farther away." He smiled

Suddenly he saw it. Big, dark.
Then he heard Peggy scream.

to himself. Peggy was a good sport. He knew she was scared. But she sure was trying not to show it.

"Did you hear something?" Peggy called out.

"Shhh. Listen." Brett thought he had heard voices. He squinted into the fog on one side of the boat—then the other. Not a sound except for the lapping of the water against the boat.

Suddenly he saw it. Big and dark and close. Then he heard Peggy's scream.

Chapter 4

Sinking

It was too late to turn the boat. Brett yelled, "Hang on, Peggy. We're going to smash."

The big, dark fishing boat loomed over them like a shadow. The men on the fishing boat yelled, "Get out of the way!"

Helpless, Brett watched in horror as the boat bore down upon them. He felt the first jolt. Then the shaking of the sailboat—and the smell of fish—the sound of wood and plastic splintering—and voices screaming. Was one of the voices Peggy's?

Then Brett felt the icy water as he was pitched into the bay. The water covered his head. His mouth tasted of salt water. His glasses were gone.

Where was Peggy? The water was freezing. His heart pounded in panic. He looked around wildly. A board floated by. He reached for it and hung on.

Then he felt a warmness in his legs and body. His eyes felt heavy. Voices sounded far away. His whole body seemed to be relaxed. He heard his name. Someone was calling him. He wanted to answer. But he was so tired.

But he couldn't go to sleep. He had to find Peggy. He forced himself to stay awake. Then he heard a yell, "I can't find Jake. He's overboard. Man overboard!" Other voices cried, "Throw him a line."

Were they talking about him? No, his name wasn't Jake. Must be one of the fishermen from the boat that rammed them. Jake wouldn't last long in this icy water without a board to help him float, Brett thought. He held on tighter to his board. Then he thought about Peggy. Had she been thrown into the water, too? Panic filled him, and he tried to see through the fog. He forced himself to listen. To try to hear Peggy's soft voice over the fishermen's shouts.

Then he heard a moan. Was it Peggy? He held onto the board and kicked toward what was left of the sailboat. He could barely see without his glasses. But he could feel. He could hear. And he could yell. He'd find her.

He was alongside the boat now. He heard a

20

sound. Peggy!

"Are you all right?" Brett asked.

"Brett! I'm so glad you're all right."

Brett could barely see her. She was bunched up against the far side of the boat. "You have your Mae West life vest on, don't you?"

"Yes."

"Take your time and climb over the side of the boat."

"Get in the water?" Her voice rose.

"Sure. It's not bad at all. And I'm here. Right beside you." Brett tried to make his voice sound strong.

"But—but what about things that bite?"

"That's the least of our troubles." Brett spoke sharply. He had to get her out of the boat. It was going to sink and the suction might pull her down. "Come on, Peggy. You can do it."

"Can't I just wait? Maybe someone will come along and tow the boat in." Peggy's voice shook.

"Listen. This isn't any freeway. Get out of the boat. NOW." He hoped she'd obey. Because now he had another problem. He was bleeding. The water was pinkish around him. It must be his leg. When he first hit the water, he had felt pain just below the knee. Now the leg felt numb.

She didn't move. He could almost smell her

fear. Somehow, some way he had to get himself in the boat. With him beside her maybe she'd go over the side. Would the sailboat stay afloat long enough? And more than that, could he keep from passing out long enough to save her and himself?

Chapter 5

Abandon Ship

The boat leaned to one side. So Brett swam around to the other side. He was sure that with his weight the lower side would take on more water.

He let go of the board and grabbed the rim of the boat. The boat tipped to his side.

"Brett! You're going to tip it over. Stop!" Peggy cried.

"Take it easy. I'm going to climb in." He tried to pull himself up. But his arms felt heavy and useless. Three times he grabbed the rim. Three times he got part of the way up. Three times he splashed back into the bay.

He felt light-headed. And without his glasses everything was blurred. Now the men's voices from the fishing boat seemed to be fading. Was he about to pass out? He had to stay awake long enough to get Peggy out of the sinking boat.

He grabbed the rim again. This time he threw his left leg over the edge. He hung on. Not willing to fall back into the water. Not able to climb into the boat.

"Blood! You're hurt."

Brett felt Peggy's tug. She held onto his belt and pulled. He tumbled into the boat. His weight caused the boat to sink lower in the water.

He heard a ripping sound and opened his eyes. What was Peggy tearing?

She leaned down beside him. "Let me wrap that cut. It's really bleeding, Brett." She pulled up his pants leg. "Oh, oh!"

"Bad gash, huh?" he asked.

"Yeah. But I'll make this shirt-tail bandage tight. That'll probably stop the bleeding." Her voice sounded calm.

After his leg had been bandaged, Brett scooted himself onto the seat. "Thanks, Peggy. Already it feels better."

"I'm scared, Brett. What are we going to do?" Her voice trembled.

"We're going to get out of this sinking boat. That's what we're going to do." He explained that the suction might pull them down.

"Can't we just wait for help? See. The fog isn't as bad. I can see the fishing boat. Maybe someone will come looking for us." She stopped, then added. "I got it. The two-way radio in the galley. We could send a message!"

"We could. But the galley's underwater. Even if we could get to the radio, it would be wet. Wouldn't work. Believe me, Peggy, the safest thing for us to do is abandon ship. I'll lower you

"That'll probably stop the bleeding."

down. Grab that board that's floating nearby. Then I'll join you."

Brett checked her Mae West life vest. He grabbed the life preserver. "I'll toss this to you, too."

Finally Peggy was overboard. But she still hung onto the rim.

"Here's the life preserver. Now let go."

She grabbed the preserver with one hand. It slipped over her arm. Then she let go.

Brett watched her go under water. Then she bobbed to the top. She was coughing and sputtering. He let himself over the side of the boat and dropped into the water.

Peggy grabbed him around the neck. He heard her sobs. She was terrified. He tried to loosen her hold on him. She'd drown both of them if he didn't get her calmed down.

"Let go, Peggy." With one hand he pried at her fingers. "You're all right. I can't help you if you don't ease up."

Now her legs were wrapped around him. His head went under water. He tried to push away from her, but she held onto him with all her strength. The loss of blood from the gash on his leg had drained him. He knew there was no way he could overpower a terrified and struggling victim. He had to get to the surface. He had to get air. He reached out and pinched her arm. With a cry of pain she let go and he swam a few feet from her. When he was sure she was calm and thinking clearly, he joined her. Now they floated side by side in the water.

The men from the fishing boat were still looking for the man who had fallen overboard. Two men in a rubber boat paddled by Peggy and Brett. "Are you guys all right?" one of the men asked.

"Yeah. Cold, but OK."

"Hey, captain," the man yelled up to a man on the deck of the fishing boat. "Throw down that extra rubber boat." The man started to paddle away. "After you're in the boat, the captain will drop you some blankets." He called his shipmate's name again. "Jake. Hey, Jake."

Brett wished the captain would hurry up with that rubber boat. Peggy's teeth were chattering. Then he heard a plop. The rubber boat bobbed at the side of the fishing boat.

"Come on, Peggy. Paddle over to the boat. I'll help you in."

He pushed the rubber boat tight against the fishing vessel. Then he shoved Peggy over the side into it.

"Give me your hand, Brett. I'll help you."

Brett raised his hand. But now it seemed so dark. Was it night? Now the voices of the men sounded loud. There was a buzzing in his head. Was it a motor boat? Putt-putt-putt.

Peggy held tight to his hand. If he could just rest a moment.

Then he heard the shout. The word clanged in his head.

"SHARK! SHARK! SHARK!"

Chapter 6

Attack!

Brett could see the look of horror on Peggy's face. He wanted to say something that would help. But it was all he could do to hang on to the side of the rubber boat.

"Shark, Brett. A shark. You've got to get in the boat. Try to lift yourself up." Peggy pulled at his arm.

He tried. He tried again. But his legs felt as if they had weights on them.

"Oh my gosh!" Peggy's voice was a terrified whisper. "The fin. The shark's fin. It's like a knife blade slicing the water . . . Brett, come on. Get in the boat."

The shark swam around the fishing boat. Then it went around the sinking sailboat.

Now the men from the fishing boat were yelling. "Get out of the water. Shark. Shark! Shark!"

Brett's heart pounded. He heard the panic in the men's voices. He knew that sharks were drawn by blood. Again he struggled to pull himself over the side of the boat. Then he heard Peggy scream.

"It's coming! It's coming!"

Brett moved to the end of the rubber boat. The shark's fin showed just above the water. It was heading right for him.

Like slow motion he watched it come closer and closer. He wondered when his life would pass before his eyes. He had heard that's what happened just before a person died. He wished he had mowed the lawn. Dad had asked him to. But he had promised to do it after sailing. Now the shark was so close, he could almost touch it. And Dad would have to mow the lawn. Brett looked up at Peggy in the boat.

She had picked up the paddle. She stood watching the shark. When the shark was just a few feet away, she crashed the paddle down on its back. The shark turned. Brett watched as it swam through the water away from the rubber boat.

"It's gone, Brett. Try to climb in." Peggy said.

Brett wanted to get in. More than anything—because he knew the shark would be back. Again he tried to lift himself into the boat. The boat tipped dangerously. This time Peggy didn't cry out.

"You've got to do it, Brett. That shark might come back."

Then they heard a shout. "We found him. We found Jake! Pull him aboard." The fisherman

When the shark was just a few feet away,
she crashed the paddle down.

sounded as if he were crying. "Come on, Jake. Up you come. Lucky we found you. A shark is close. Must smell blood."

"Brett! You can do it. Come on. I'll help." Peggy was on her knees. She leaned over the edge of the boat.

Brett looked up. If he weren't so scared, he'd have laughed. Those crazy underwater goggles hung around her neck.

"What are you smiling about? This is not funny. The shark!" Her voice sounded wild.

"Your goggles." He wanted to explain but it was too much effort.

He heard a splash. Was it the shark? He closed his eyes. He didn't want to see.

Chapter 7

Drifting

Brett heard Peggy's voice. "You can do it. I'll shove. Grab hold of the rim and pull yourself up."

Panic grabbed him. What was she doing in the water? He must be dreaming. Peggy wouldn't get in the water. She was terrified of deep water. He felt a jerk on his belt.

"Go for it, Brett. I'll push. You can do it."

It was Peggy. She was in the water beside him. Now he was angry. Angry that he'd done his best to protect her. And she'd jumped in. How was he going to save her now? It was all he could do to hold onto the boat himself. Why didn't she save herself and forget about him?

"Listen to me, Brett." Peggy pinched his arm hard. "We've got to hurry. Get in the boat fast. Now go for it!"

He grabbed hold of the rim and lifted. Peggy

had a hold of one leg and was pushing. He threw his hurt leg over the edge. He teetered. She shoved. He sprawled on the bottom of the boat.

Then he heard the men from the fishing boat shouting. "Shark. It's coming. Get her out of the water."

He sat up. Peggy held on to the rim of the boat.

"Get out of the way, Brett. Here I come." She lifted herself up — just like he'd seen her do on the gym bar — arms straight, head high. Then she threw her leg over the side.

Brett stood up and grabbed the paddle. Peggy tumbled into the boat. The fin of the shark was within ten feet of them. He raised the paddle. Ready.

The shark headed for the rubber boat. Then it suddenly changed its course. It passed between the sinking sailboat and the fishing boat.

"Whew! That was close." Brett fell weakly onto a seat. He was sweating and shaking."

"You guys all right?" a voice from the fishing boat yelled down.

"We're OK."

"We're dropping a couple of blankets. Wrap yourselves up. Then paddle away from these boats as fast as you can. They're going down.

They could take you with them." In a few moments two blankets were lowered.

Brett handed Peggy a blanket. "Wrap up. Then grab a paddle and we'll get away from here."

He wrapped the other blanket around himself. He didn't feel as dizzy as he had in the water.

"We're leaving our boat," a man from the fishing vessel yelled down. "We've called the Coast Guard. They're coming for us — if they can find us in this blasted fog."

"Thanks for the blankets," Peggy called.

"Let's try to keep our boats together. It will make it easier for the Coast Guard," the man said.

"Right," Brett answered.

Peggy held a paddle. "Ready, Brett?"

"Ready." He dipped the paddle into the water. They pulled away from the fishing boat.

"We got away just in time, didn't we?" Peggy said. She paddled smoothly.

Now they saw the fishermen in another rubber boat shove off from the fishing boat. They were't wasting any time getting away from the suction of the sinking boats.

Minutes later there was a rumble. The mast from the sailboat cracked and fell into the water.

Moments later, the sailboat sank.

Brett swallowed hard. The lump in his throat wouldn't go down. The boat held many happy memories. Now those memories rested on the ocean floor.

Peggy reached out and touched his arm. "I'm sorry, Brett. I know it hurts to lose your ship."

"*Boat,* Peggy. It was a sailboat." He knew he was being cranky. But it helped to cover up his hurt.

"Whatever — I'm sorry," she said softly.

He smiled at her. "Thanks. And, Peggy, you were great. You saved my life."

"I saved *me.* No way was I going to row around without a real sailor by my side." She pulled his pant leg up. "How's the leg?"

"It hurts but it's stopped bleeding."

"Look! The fishing boat. It's going down." Peggy turned to watch.

The big boat rattled and rumbled. It seemed to struggle to stay afloat. There was a sucking noise. Then it disappeared beneath the water. The waves rocked their small rubber boat.

"I see what you mean about being pulled down. Even this far away we can feel the rough water," Peggy said.

"Hey, we'd better get paddling. Those

36

fishermen are almost out of sight," Brett said. "The fog seems to be lifting some. But it would be easy to lose them."

They paddled silently for awhile. It wasn't easy but they kept the fishermen's boat in sight.

Brett's leg hurt more and more. The effort of paddling had started the bleeding again. Fresh blood soaked the blanket around his legs. Then he heard Peggy's gasp.

"They're gone. One minute they were just ahead of us. Now they're gone. The fishermen are gone!"

"It's the fog. They've disappeared into a fog bank," Brett said.

"Or sank." Peggy's voice shook. "We're all alone now. How is anybody going to find us? We're just a black dot bobbing around in dark waters."

"Hey, stop worrying. We've got it good now. We're safe in a boat. We have blankets. And the Coast Guard's been called." Brett tried to sound sure.

"But, Brett, what if our boat gets a leak? What if we sink—like maybe those fishermen did? What if night comes . . ."

"Paddle." Brett said firmly. "We'll spot them again. I know we will." But fear made it hard for him to breathe.

"How will the Coast Guard find us now?" Peggy asked.

"Paddle, Peggy. I've checked my compass. We're heading in the right direction." Brett didn't tell her that the ocean water might have ruined the compass. She already had plenty to worry about.

Chapter 8

Rescue

Now the water became choppy again. Brett steered the rubber boat through the rough water. The boat rode a wave up and then was tossed about on the wave going down.

He looked at Peggy. Her mouth was closed tight — as if she were holding back a scream. He wanted to pat her hand and tell her not to worry. The Coast Guard would come soon. But it was hard to lie when he was scared, too.

The fog blocked out any landmarks. He wasn't sure if his compass was working. Brett wondered if they were on their way out to sea.

He had another worry. His leg. He was losing a lot of blood now. What would Peggy do if he passed out?

The waves seemed bigger now. The little boat rocked higher and higher. Brett saw that Peggy held her breath each time the boat rose. And let it out when the boat reached the bottom of the wave.

"What time is it, Brett?" Peggy asked.

"Why? You got a big date waiting?" Brett teased.

Peggy laughed. It was a shaky laugh. "You're my big date. What time is it?"

The boat rode a wave up and then was tossed about on a wave going down.

"My watch stopped. It's water-proof and shock-proof. But not shipwreck proof." Brett was quiet a moment. Then he added, "But we left Shepherd Island around two. And I guess we've been on the water about two hours. That makes it around four o'clock. That's just a rough guess, Peggy."

"At least it's still light," Peggy said. Then she looked down at Brett's leg. "You're bleeding. Right through the blanket!"

"Yeah. It began again when I started paddling. Guess the strain makes it bleed," Brett said.

She laid the blanket back and pulled up his pant leg. "Brett, you're losing too much blood. You've got to lie down and put your leg up. I can paddle for both of us. You just keep me going in the right direction."

Brett wanted to lie down. He was so tired. Peggy helped him lie down on the bottom of the boat. The boat wasn't long enough for him to stretch out all the way. Peggy said, "That's good. Now put your leg up on the seat."

She jerked her shirt loose and ripped a strip from the bottom. Then she took off the old bandage. She wrapped the fresh strip around the gash on his leg. She tucked the blanket around him.

He lay with his head propped against the boat. His leg rested on the seat next to Peggy.

"There. Now keep an eye on me, captain. I don't want to be the first person to paddle to China!"

Brett laughed. She was some girl. Not very big. Not much of a sailor. But she knew how to hang in there. It felt good to rest. Maybe in a little while the bleeding would stop. He could take his turn at paddling.

He didn't know how long it'd been. He must have dozed off. But Peggy was calling him.

"Wake up, Brett. I hear something," she said.

He held his breath and listened. Then he heard it. His hopes dropped. "Sorry, Peggy. It's only a bird looking for food."

"Oh, sorry I woke you." Peggy sounded let down.

He must try to stay awake. Keep her hopes up. But he must have dozed off again. Suddenly something brought him full awake. A sound. He lay quietly waiting. He hoped it wasn't a dream. There it was again. A fog horn!

"Peggy! Did you hear that!" He half sat up.

"It's not another bird, is it?" she asked.

"Nope. That's a fog horn!"

"A fog horn! That's the nicest sound I ever

heard. Do you think it's the Coast Guard?"

"Doesn't matter who it is. Someone is out in this fog with us."

The horn blared again.

"Here! Here!" Brett yelled out. Peggy yelled, too.

"Hold on," a voice from the fog called. "We're coming."

Suddenly a boat slid through the fog. In minutes the Coast Guard cutter was beside them.

Brett made sure that Peggy was lifted to safety first. After all, he *was* the captain. Even if his ship did go down.

Moments later they both were in the Coast Guard cutter.

Soon they were in dry clothes and drinking hot coffee. Brett's leg had a fresh bandage. "Well, so far, how do you like sailing?" Brett asked Peggy.

The men of the Coast Guard laughed. Peggy just smiled.

"A message just came. They've picked up the men from the fishing boat," a crew man reported.

Brett took a deep breath. "That's great. All's well that ends well. Right, Peggy?"

"Ends? What do you mean, captain? We've just begun. I'm going to be the best sailing partner you've ever had."

"Honest? You mean you'd go out sailing again?" He grinned. All she needed was time. She'd make a great sailor.

"Aye, aye, captain." Peggy put on her underwater goggles. With a snappy salute she said, "Ready and willing to serve on your ship."

"*Boat!*" Brett said.

"Whatever."